Leroy Ninker
Saddles Up

Books for early readers
FROM KATE DICAMILLO AND CHRIS VAN DUSEN

Mercy Watson
Mercy Watson to the Rescue
Mercy Watson Goes for a Ride
Mercy Watson Fights Crime
Mercy Watson: Princess in Disguise
Mercy Watson Thinks Like a Pig
Mercy Watson: Something Wonky This Way Comes

Tales from Deckawoo Drive
Leroy Ninker Saddles Up
Francine Poulet Meets the Ghost Racoon

Tales from Deckawoo Drive

Volume One

Leroy Ninker Saddles Up

Kate DiCamillo

illustrated by Chris Van Dusen

CANDLEWICK PRESS

Text copyright © 2014 by Kate DiCamillo
Illustrations copyright © 2014 by Chris Van Dusen

First paperback edition 2015

Library of Congress Catalog Card Number 2013953473
ISBN 978-0-7636-6339-1 (hardcover)
ISBN 978-0-7636-8012-1 (paperback)

15 16 17 18 19 20 BVG 10 9 8 7 6 5 4 3 2 1

Printed in Berryville, VA, U.S.A.

This book was typeset in Mrs. Eaves.
The illustrations were done in gouache.

Candlewick Press
99 Dover Street
Somerville, Massachusetts 02144

visit us at www.candlewick.com

To Amy and her class of heroes
K. D. and C. V.

Chapter One

Leroy Ninker worked at the Bijou Drive-In Theater concession stand.

It was Leroy's job to pour drinks and butter popcorn and smile a very large smile.

At the concession stand, Leroy Ninker said, "Thank you very much!"

He said, "Extra butter on that?"

He also said, "Yippie-i-oh."

Leroy Ninker said "Yippie-i-oh" because Leroy Ninker had a dream. He wanted to be a cowboy.

On Wednesday nights, the Bijou Drive-In Theater ran a Western double feature, and Leroy Ninker stood and watched in wonder as the great white expanse of the Bijou screen filled with purple mountains, wide-open plains, and cowboys.

The cowboys wore ten-gallon hats. They wore boots. They carried lassos. The cowboys were men who cast long shadows and knew how to fight injustice. They were men who were never, ever afraid.

"Yippie-i-oh," Leroy Ninker whispered to the screen. "That is the life for me. A cowboy is who I was meant to be."

2

"Who are you whispering to?" said Beatrice Leapaleoni.

Beatrice was the ticket seller at the Bijou. Once all the tickets were sold and the movie had begun, Beatrice joined Leroy Ninker in the concession stand so that she could eat popcorn and watch the movie.

"I am not whispering," said Leroy Ninker very loudly. "Cowboys do not whisper."

"Can I make a point?" said Beatrice Leapaleoni. "Can I make a simple observation?"

"Yes," said Leroy.

"All these cowboys," said Beatrice, "what have they got?"

"Hats," said Leroy Ninker as he stared at the screen. "And also boots."

"Yep," said Beatrice. "What else?"

"Lassos," said Leroy. He put his hand on his lasso.

"And?" said Beatrice.

"Tracking abilities?" said Leroy.

Beatrice heaved a heavy sigh. "I am thinking of something that you can actually see. Something right in front of you." She paused. "Something that the cowboys are sitting on."

Leroy Ninker took off his hat and scratched his head.

Beatrice sighed again. "Horses, Leroy," she said. "Every cowboy needs a horse."

Leroy Ninker was a small man with a big dream. He was also the kind of man who knew the truth when he heard it. Suddenly, his hat and his lasso and his boots and his *yippie-i-oh*s didn't feel like enough. Beatrice Leapaleoni was right. How could he ever hope to be a cowboy, a real cowboy, a true cowboy, without a horse?

"Yep," said Beatrice, "you've got a problem. You've got to procure a horse. But don't worry, I happen to have the solution for you right here." She held up a copy of the *Gizzford Gazette*. "Listen,"

6

she said. Beatrice adjusted her glasses. She cleared her throat.

"'Horse for sale,'" Beatrice Leapaleoni read. "'Old but good. Very exceptionally cheap.'"

HORSE FoR SALE

"Yippie-i-oh," said Leroy Ninker. He took out his wallet and counted his money. He looked at Beatrice Leapaleoni. He said, "How much is very exceptionally cheap?"

"I guess you won't know until you ask," said Beatrice.

"Right," said Leroy. He counted his money again. "I hope I have enough."

"Listen," said Beatrice. "What you have to do here is take fate in your hands and wrestle it to the ground."

"Right!" said Leroy. "I am going to wrestle fate. I am going to get a horse!"

"There you go," said Beatrice. She tore the ad out of the paper and handed it to Leroy.

"Yippie-i-oh," said Leroy. He carefully folded the piece of paper and put it in his wallet.

"Don't forget to inspect the teeth," said Beatrice Leapaleoni. "And the hooves. That is what matters with horses. Teeth. And hooves."

"Teeth and hooves," said Leroy Ninker.

"Exactly," said Beatrice.

★　★　★

That night, Leroy Ninker did not sleep well. He dreamed of horses. Specifically, he dreamed of teeth and hooves.

Also, he dreamed of Beatrice Leapa-leoni. In his dream, she kept clearing her throat and saying, "Take fate in your hands, take fate in your hands, take fate in your hands."

"And then what?" said Leroy Ninker in the dream.

"And then," said Beatrice Leapaleoni in a very solemn voice, "you must wrestle it to the ground."

Chapter Two

The next morning after breakfast, Leroy Ninker put his hat on his head and his boots on his feet. He consulted the ad from the *Gizzford Gazette*. He read aloud the address of the horse for sale.

"'Route sixteen, third house on the left,'" said Leroy Ninker. And then he said it again, "Route sixteen, third house on the left," just to make sure he had it right.

Leroy folded the ad back up. He put it in his wallet. He adjusted his hat. He was now prepared to take fate in his hands and wrestle it to the ground. He was ready to procure a horse. Leroy set out walking.

The sun was high above his head, and the sky was very blue. As Leroy walked, he imagined that he was on the open plain.

A car drove by. "Look, Mama!" A boy in the backseat of the car pointed at Leroy. "It's a very tiny cowboy."

Leroy stood up straighter.

"I am a cowboy on his way to procure a horse," he said. "I am a man wrestling fate to the ground."

Another car drove by. Someone threw a can out the window. The can hit Leroy Ninker in the head.

"Dang nib it," said Leroy. He stopped
and took off his hat. He rubbed at his
head. "Don't get agitated," he told himself.
"Just keep thinking about your horse."

Leroy Ninker put his hat back on his
head and started walking again. He thought
about his horse. *I hope he is a fast horse,* he
thought. *And I hope that he is strong. I will call
him Tornado.*

Leroy found this name so pleasing that he had to stop walking and hold himself very still and properly consider the glory of the word.

"Tornado," Leroy whispered.

And then he shouted it: *"Tornado!"*

It was the most perfect name for a horse ever.

"Tornado!" shouted Leroy Ninker again. "Yippie-i-oh."

The cowboy started to run. He was heading to meet the horse of his dreams! There was no time to waste!

"I'm on my way, Tornado!" shouted Leroy Ninker as he ran down the side of the road.

By the time Leroy made it to his destination, it was late afternoon and his feet hurt.

"What can I do for you?" said the woman who answered the door.

"I am here about the horse," said Leroy.

"You're interested in Maybelline?" said the woman.

"Maybelline?" said Leroy.

"Follow me, Hank," said the woman.

"Hank?" said Leroy.

The woman walked to the back of the house. Leroy followed her. "Since you are asking," said the woman over her shoulder, "my name is Patty LeMarque. Maybelline is right over here."

Patty LeMarque climbed a fence.

Leroy climbed the fence, too.

"There she is," said Patty LeMarque. She waved her arm in the direction of a horse standing in a field. "There is Maybelline."

At the sound of her name, the horse turned and came trotting toward them. She whinnied. She was a big horse, and her whinny was very loud.

"Maybelline," said Patty LeMarque, "meet Hank."

The horse whinnied again. She opened her mouth wide. Leroy took advantage of her mouth being open to look at her teeth. There weren't a lot of them. As far as he could tell, there were four in total.

How many teeth was a horse supposed to have? Beatrice Leapaleoni had not said.

Leroy Ninker looked down at the horse's hooves. There were four of them, too.

That seemed good.

"Yippie-i-oh," said Leroy Ninker.

The horse put her nose right up in his face. It was a large nose. There were whiskers on it, and it smelled very much like the nose of a horse.

"She likes you," said Patty LeMarque. "Ain't that something? Maybelline don't like everybody. In fact, there's a whole raft of people she don't like. She is a particular horse, if you don't mind me saying so."

"I don't mind you saying so," said Leroy.

He put out his hand and touched the horse's nose. It was damp and velvety. Leroy felt his heart tumble and roll inside of him. Oh, to be a cowboy with a horse! To ride into the sunset! To ride into the wind! To be brave and true and cast a large, horsey shadow!

"Maybelline," said Leroy Ninker.

"That's her name," said Patty LeMarque.

"I'll take her," said Leroy.

Chapter Three

"Now, Maybelline's old," said Patty LeMarque, "and I am moving, and where I am moving to, they don't take horses. My main goal here is to make sure that Maybelline goes to a home where she is loved up good through all her older, more golden years. You understand what I'm saying, Hank?"

"Yippie-i-oh," said Leroy.

"I ain't looking for money is what I am saying. I am looking for love for Maybelline. And I am just going on my instinctuals here, but my instinctuals tell me that you are the right little fellow for this horse. So now I am going to tell you some things about Maybelline. Listen up, Hank."

"Yippie-i-oh," said Leroy.

Patty LeMarque looked at him. She squinted. "I don't know what that means, Hank," she said.

"Okay," said Leroy. "It means okay."

"If okay is what you mean, Hank," said Patty LeMarque, "then just flat out say it. Be a straightforward communicator, like me."

"Okay," said Leroy.

"Okay!" said Patty LeMarque. "Here are the things about Maybelline. There are three items you got to remember. Item one is that she is the kind of horse who enjoys the heck out of a compliment. You got to talk sweet to Maybelline, understand?"

"Yippie-i-oh," said Leroy.

"Itchie-pitchie-poo, Hank," said Patty LeMarque. "Say what you mean and mean what you say."

"Okay," said Leroy.

"There you go!" said Patty LeMarque. "Item two about Maybelline is that she is a horse who eats a lot of grub. And when I say a lot of grub, I mean something real specified. What I mean is this horse eats A. Lot. Of. Grub."

"Okay," said Leroy. He nodded. "A lot of grub."

"Item three is that Maybelline is the kind of horse who gets lonesome quick. What I mean by that is that she is not the kind of horse who cares to be left behind. This is the most important item, Hank. Do not leave Maybelline alone for long, or you will live to rue and regret the day."

"Rue and regret the day," said Leroy. "Okay."

"All right, then," said Patty LeMarque. "She's all saddled up and ready to go. Let me give you a hand here, Hank, since you are kind of a short little gentleman who looks to be in need of assistance with some of life's more overwhelming necessities."

Patty LeMarque helped Leroy Ninker up on Maybelline's back, and right away Leroy Ninker noticed that the world was different from the top of a horse. The colors were deeper. The sun shone brighter. The birds sang more sweetly.

Also, Patty LeMarque seemed shorter and a tiny bit less bossy.

"Giddy-up," said Leroy Ninker to his horse.

Nothing happened.

Leroy Ninker slapped the reins. "Giddy-up," he said again.

Maybelline stood without moving.

"Hank," said Patty LeMarque, "I don't believe that you were listening to me even one tiny bit when I listed out them three items. You got to listen in this world, Hank. You got to pay attention to the informational bits that people share with you."

"Okay," said Leroy.

"Okay, then. Listen up. If I were you, I would cogitate on item one right about now."

"Do what?" said Leroy.

"Compliment her," whispered Patty LeMarque. "Give the horse some pretty words."

Leroy Ninker looked down at Maybelline's bony back. He counted the knobs in her spine. He tried to think of some pretty words. Did he even know any pretty words?

Leroy thought very hard.

And finally, Leroy spoke. He opened his mouth and said the sweetest words he could think of. He said, "You are the most beautified horse in the whole wide green world."

The horse pricked up her ears. She twitched the left ear to the right and the right ear to the left. Both ears quivered hopefully.

Emboldened, Leroy Ninker leaned forward and spoke directly into the right ear. He said, "You are the sweetest blossom in springtime."

Maybelline picked up her right front hoof. She held it high in the air.

"Good job, Hank," said Patty LeMarque.

"You are a pure flower of horsiness!" said Leroy Ninker.

Maybelline began to walk.

"Well, look at you, Hank," said Patty LeMarque. "It seems you got a talent for poeticals."

"Oh, Maybelline!" shouted Leroy. "You are the brightest star in the velvety nighttime sky!"

Maybelline broke into a trot.

"Good-bye, Maybelline!" shouted Patty LeMarque. "Good luck, Hank. Remember them other two items! And listen to the people of the world when they offer you informational bits!"

Patty LeMarque held up a hand and waved, and Leroy waved back and then Patty LeMarque disappeared.

Maybelline (Leroy's horse!) was going very, very fast.

Chapter Four

Leroy Ninker held on tight. He thought of more pretty words, and he said them.

"Sweetness," said the cowboy. "Lovely one. Beloved."

The horse went faster.

"Maybelline of my dreams!" shouted Leroy Ninker.

The world was a green and gold blur, and Leroy was happier than he had ever been in his life. Maybelline ran and ran and ran.

The horse ran until the sun was low in the sky and the shadows were long and sad.

"Maybelline," said Leroy into Maybelline's left ear, "it is time for the two of us to head home."

Maybelline nickered. She slowed down to a trot. And then she stopped entirely. Leroy Ninker slid forward in the saddle.

"Giddy-up, my beautiful one," said Leroy.

But Maybelline held still.

"Yippie-i-oh, my beloved," said Leroy. "We are homeward bound."

Maybelline looked to the left, and then she looked to the right. She let out a long whinny.

"Oh," said Leroy. "I get it." He slid off Maybelline's back. He took hold of the reins. "Come on, horse of my heart," he said. "I will show you the way home."

Leroy walked ahead, and Maybelline followed behind, and every once in a while, she would give Leroy a friendly little bump with her nose, pushing him forward. And in this way, the cowboy and his horse made their way home through the deepening purple dusk.

Home was the Garden Glen Apartments, Unit 12.

Unit 12 was a very small apartment, which was just fine because Leroy was a very small man. Maybelline, however, was not a small horse. She was a tall horse and she was a wide horse, and she would not fit through the door of Unit 12.

"Gol' dang it," said Leroy Ninker.

He gave Maybelline a little push. And when that didn't work, he gave her a large shove. But Leroy soon saw that it was impossible. All the shoving in the world was not going to make Maybelline fit through the door of Unit 12.

"Dag blibber it," said Leroy. He actually felt like he might cry. Which was ridiculous because cowboys definitely did not cry.

Leroy closed his eyes, and Patty LeMarque's face floated into view. She opened her mouth and said, "Cogitate on item one if you care to move forward, Hank. You got to compliment the heck out of her!"

Leroy opened his eyes. He cleared his throat. He said, "Maybelline, you are the best squeeziest-into-a-small-spot horse that I have ever known."

Maybelline twitched her ears to the left and to the right, and while the horse was busy savoring the compliment, Leroy gave her a hopeful shove.

But Maybelline still wouldn't fit through the door.

"Flibber gibber it," said Leroy. He closed his eyes and conjured up Patty LeMarque's face again. He tried to remember the other items about Maybelline. He thought very hard.

"I got it," he said. "Item two is that you are the kind of horse who eats a lot of grub."

Leroy opened his eyes.

Maybelline was looking at him in an extremely hopeful manner.

"Well, yippie-i-okay," said Leroy Ninker. "I will make us some food, and then we will deal with the too-small door."

Maybelline looked as overjoyed as it was possible for a horse to look, and Leroy was moved to compliment her again.

"You are the most splendiferous horse in all of creation," he said.

Maybelline whinnied long and loud. She nodded in agreement.

She truly was an excellent horse.

Leroy didn't think he would ever be done admiring her.

Chapter Five

Leroy Ninker went into the kitchen of Unit 12. He opened the refrigerator and looked inside.

Leroy had viewed many, many Westerns at the Bijou Drive-In Theater. He had seen a great deal of purple mountains and wide-open plains. He had watched cowboys battling injustices and crossing rivers and eating beans.

But he could not recall one movie where
a cowboy said aloud exactly what it was that
he was feeding to his horse.

"Hay?" said Leroy. He lifted up his hat
and scratched his head. "Oats?"

But he didn't have hay. And he didn't
have oats.

"Dag flibber it," said Leroy Ninker.

Outside of Unit 12, Maybelline let out a long, loud whinny that had a question mark on the end of it.

"Okay!" Leroy shouted to the horse. "I am making you some grub! Yippie-i-oh."

Leroy grabbed a big pot and filled it with water. He turned the heat on high. He filled another pot with tomato sauce.

Patty LeMarque had said nothing about whether or not Maybelline liked spaghetti, but didn't everyone like spaghetti?

After Leroy Ninker added the noodles to the pot, he went outside and leaned up against his horse. Her flank was very warm. She was an extremely comforting horse to lean against.

Maybelline turned her head and looked at Leroy, and then she put her nose up in the air and sniffed.

"That's right," said Leroy. "I am cooking you some grub."

Maybelline whinnied.

"It's spaghetti," said Leroy. "I hope you like spaghetti."

It turned out that Maybelline did like spaghetti.

She liked a lot of spaghetti.

The horse ate the first pot of noodles in a single gigantic gulp. As far as Leroy could tell, she didn't even bother to chew.

When she was done, Maybelline lifted her head from the pot and looked at Leroy in a meaningful way. Leroy said, "Yippie-i-oh," and he went running back into Unit 12 with the empty pot and started boiling more water. He opened another jar of tomato sauce. He made a second pot of spaghetti.

After that, he made a third pot of spaghetti.

By the time Maybelline was done eating, the stars were shining in the sky and the moon was looking down and there was not one noodle of spaghetti left in Unit 12.

Leroy Ninker was very tired. He leaned against his horse and looked up at the stars. But when he closed his eyes, what he saw was Patty LeMarque. Her face was as big as the moon, and her mouth was opening and closing, and opening and closing.

Leroy knew exactly what she was saying.

Patty LeMarque was reciting item three.

"Maybelline?" said Leroy.

Maybelline turned and put her nose in Leroy's face.

"I have remembered item three," said Leroy Ninker. "Item three is that you are the kind of horse who gets lonesome quick."

Maybelline nickered.

"But you cannot fit inside Unit 12," said Leroy.

Maybelline shook her head.

"Okay, then," said Leroy. "I will stay here with you."

He took off his boots. He removed his lasso. He loosened his belt. And then he lay down at Maybelline's feet. He put his hat over his eyes. He sighed a happy sigh.

"I have made a lot of mistakes in my life," said Leroy Ninker from underneath his hat. "I have done some things that I wish I had not done. I have taken some wrong turns."

There was a long silence. Leroy moved his hat and looked up at Maybelline. The horse looked down at him. She was listening.

"There was a time in my life when I was a thief," said Leroy. "I am now reformed.

46

I hope you don't judge me, Maybelline, because I truly am a changed man."

Maybelline let out a small chuff of air.

"Oh, Maybelline," said Leroy. "You are my horse. For me, you shine brighter than every star and every planet. You shine brighter than all the universe's moons and suns. There are not enough *yippie-i-oh*s to describe you, Maybelline. I love you."

Leroy Ninker had never imagined that he could string so many words together at once. It was the longest speech of his life.

He looked up at Maybelline, and she looked down at him. Leroy's cheeks felt hot. He lowered his hat so that it covered his face. "Good night, Maybelline," he whispered.

Leroy closed his eyes. He thought very hard.

Had his heart been waiting for Maybelline to come along so that it could open wide and he could speak all the beautiful words that had been hiding inside of him?

It was an amazing concept to consider, and the cowboy fell asleep considering it.

Chapter Six

Leroy Ninker dreamed that he was riding Maybelline on the open plain. In the distance there were purple mountains, and high up in the sky there was a daytime moon. The moon was looking down at Leroy and Maybelline, and it was smiling at them.

In Leroy's dream, Maybelline was running very fast.

Also, she had a full set of teeth.

It's just like a movie, thought Leroy. *We are just like a horse and cowboy in a movie.*

The wind rushed across his face. It smelled like cinnamon and clover and spaghetti sauce.

The wind is promising me wonderful things, thought Leroy.

And then he thought, *Patty LeMarque is right. I am very good at speaking poeticals.*

Maybelline's hooves pounded on the earth.

Maybelline's hooves were extremely loud. Leroy had never heard such loud hooves, even in the movies. Maybelline's hooves were as loud as thunder.

The cinnamon-and-clover-and-spaghetti-sauce-scented wind blew harder and faster. It tickled Leroy's nostrils. And then it slapped him on the cheeks. The wind, obviously, was trying to tell Leroy something important.

And then, in his dream, Leroy heard Patty LeMarque's voice. "Wake up, Hank!" she shouted. "Protect your horse!"

Leroy Ninker woke up.

Thunder crashed. A bolt of lightning lit up the world.

"Dab blibber it," said Leroy. "It's fixing to rain." He stood. He hitched up his pants and pushed his hat down on his head. He looked at Maybelline. Her eyes were closed. She was still asleep.

"Horse of my heart," whispered Leroy, "sweetest and most delicate of all springtime blossoms, I cannot let you be rained on. I will go inside and get you an umbrella."

Maybelline's eyes stayed closed.

"I'll be right back," said Leroy.

He turned and ran into Unit 12.

While Leroy was gone, the rain began. A drop fell on Maybelline's nose. Another drop fell on her ear. The horse woke up. She lifted her head and looked around her.

Terrible things were happening!

Thunder was crashing!

Lightning was flashing!

And worst of all—oh, worst of all— Maybelline was utterly, absolutely alone.

She was not the kind of horse who liked to be alone.

Maybelline let out a long, questioning whinny. The thunder crashed; the lightning flashed. Maybelline called out again.

Where was the little man? Where was the little man with the big hat and the beautiful words? Where was the little man who brought her spaghetti?

Maybelline called out again and again. There was no answer.

She didn't know what to do. And when Maybelline didn't know what to do, what Maybelline did was run.

Leroy Ninker came out of Unit 12 holding an umbrella up high over his head. "Here I am, my springtime blossom," he said, "and I have brought you an umbrella."

But when he got to where Maybelline should be, there was no Maybelline there.

"Maybelline?" said Leroy into the darkness and the wind and the rain. "Maybelline?"

The wind blew harder.

"Horse of my heart?" said Leroy Ninker.

The rain came down hard and fast. The lightning flashed, revealing a horseless world.

Leroy stared into the emptiness. He heard Patty LeMarque's voice in the wind. She was saying, "Do not leave Maybelline alone for too long, or you will live to rue and regret the day."

A great gust of wind came along and grabbed hold of Leroy's umbrella and

ripped it right out of his hands. Leroy watched as the umbrella spun up into the darkness.

He was a cowboy without a horse, a cowboy without an umbrella. He was a cowboy absolutely, utterly alone.

Chapter Seven

The cowboy walked through the dark and stormy world, shouting, "Maybelline, Maybelline, Maybelline!"

In his haste to find his horse, Leroy had left Unit 12 without his boots and without his lasso. He was not at all prepared to go on a horse search, and he had no idea where to begin.

Patty LeMarque's face appeared before him and said, "Don't forget the compliments, Hank. And the grub."

"Maybelline!" Leroy shouted. "You are the queen of yippie-i-oh-ness! You are the most beautiful horse in all of creation."

No horse appeared.

"Maybelline!" Leroy shouted. "There will be unending pots of spaghetti if only you come home to me!"

No horse appeared.

Leroy thought about Maybelline and her bony spine and her four teeth. He considered her whiskered, velvety nose. He cogitated upon her twitching, twisting ears and how she bent her head down to listen to him. Oh, she listened to him so well.

"Maybelline," Leroy whispered into the darkness, "you are the horse for me."

The rain came down harder, and the wind blew meaner. Leroy's socks were soaked through.

This is the worst night of my life, thought Leroy. *If there is anything worse than being a cowboy without a horse, it is being a cowboy who had a horse and then lost her.*

The wind howled and whistled. And then the wind grabbed hold of Leroy's hat and tossed it away.

"Dag blither it, you, you, *wind*, you . . ." Leroy shook his fist at the wind. "What am I going to do without my hat?"

Leroy Ninker was now hatless, bootless, lasso-less, and horseless.

He had never felt less like a cowboy.

"I want my horse!" Leroy Ninker shouted into the wind and rain. He sank to his knees. "Give me back my horse. Please, please. Maybelline, I promise that if I find you, I will never leave you alone again."

These words seemed so sad to Leroy that he started to cry. The wind blew stronger. The rain beat down. The world was very, very dark, and the cowboy was lost.

Oh, he was lost.

And where was the horse?

She was lost, too. She was as lost as she had ever been in her life. She was soaked to the hooves, and she was very afraid.

She was also tired.

She stopped running and held herself still in the darkness. She whinnied. And then she neighed. And then she nickered. Finally, she sighed.

The horse wanted many things. She wanted the rain to stop falling and the wind to stop howling. She wanted the little

man to appear out of the darkness holding
a gigantic pot of spaghetti.

But more than anything, Maybelline
wanted to hear the little man's voice.

The horse needed to hear some beautiful words.

But there was no little man, and there were no beautiful words. There was just darkness and rain and wind. And since Maybelline couldn't think what to do, she started to run again. She ran without thinking or hoping.

★ ★ ★

In the darkness, the horse went one way.

And the cowboy, alas, went the other.

Chapter Eight

Leroy stood in a patch of mud. He looked down at his socks. They were very dirty. He looked up at the sky. He watched as the rain slowed to a trickle. The thunder grumbled and rumbled and then slunk away. The last raindrop fell. The world became very quiet.

The sky was gray, but at the horizon, there was the slightest hint of pink.

"Dawn is coming," said Leroy Ninker. "And I do not have a hat or boots or a lasso or a horse. I don't even have an umbrella. I have nothing at all."

Leroy watched the sun slowly rise; the orange ball of it glowed brighter and brighter. He shook his head sadly. He looked down at his muddy socks again.

And then, in the pink and hopeful light of dawn, Leroy noticed something in the dirt. He bent down and traced the shape that was imprinted in the mud. His heart thumped inside of him.

"Yippie-i-oh," whispered Leroy Ninker to the hoofprint.

He looked past the first hoofprint, and he saw there was a second one and then a third.

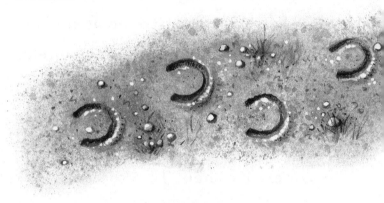

"Maybelline!" shouted Leroy Ninker.

He followed the hoofprints. He started to run. He may not have had a hat or a lasso or boots, but he was tracking a horse.

His horse.

Maybelline was out there somewhere. And a cowboy named Leroy Ninker would find her.

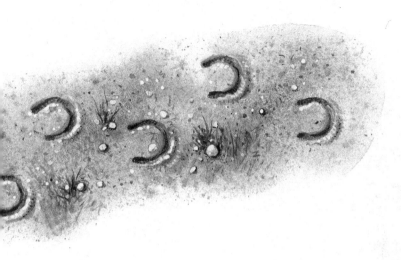

★ ★ ★

The horse was, indeed, out there somewhere. To be specific, she was three streets
over. The horse was on Deckawoo Drive.

She was standing at the window of a
house. She was watching a family sitting
down to breakfast. Wonderful, wonderful
smells were coming from inside the house,
and the family looked happy sitting together
around the table. Maybelline put her nose

very close to the window. She watched the family. She admired the food.

And when she could not bear it any longer, she raised her head and called out. She whinnied long and loud.

Leroy Ninker was following the hoofprints when he heard a sound that made him stop in his tracks. Leroy held himself very still. He listened.

He heard birdsong and the low hum of a train. He heard the whoosh of car tires on the wet pavement.

And then he heard that beautiful, singular noise again: *a whinny.* A horse. His horse. Maybelline.

Leroy ran in the direction of the whinny.

"Maybelline!" he called out. "I am on my way!"

He leaped over a bush. He ran around a bicycle. He climbed over a fence and into a backyard.

And there was Maybelline! She was standing and looking in the window of a house.

"Maybelline!" shouted Leroy.

The horse turned and looked at him. She twisted her ears left and right. Both ears trembled hopefully. It was obvious that she was waiting for some beautiful words.

Leroy's throat felt tight.

He smiled. He spread his arms wide. "Horse of my heart," he called out, "most wondrous, most glorious of all horses, I have missed you so."

Maybelline nickered. She came trotting toward him.

Leroy put his arms around her. He closed his eyes and leaned his head against her neck.

He had done it. He had taken hold of fate with both hands and wrestled it to the ground. And he had done it without a lasso, without boots, without a hat.

"Oh, Maybelline," said Leroy Ninker. "I have so many words I want to say to you."

Leroy's eyes were still closed when he heard a voice say, "Mister, is that your horse?"

Chapter Nine

Leroy Ninker opened his eyes. He saw a small girl.

"Is it?" she said. "Is that your horse?"

"Yes," said Leroy Ninker. "This is my horse. She was lost, and I tracked her through the mud. She was lost, and I found her."

"Uh-huh. What's her name?"

"Maybelline," said Leroy.

"My name is Stella," said the girl. "Can I pet your horse?"

"Yes," said Leroy Ninker. "But what this horse really likes is a compliment. Do you know how to give a compliment?"

"Of course I do," said Stella. She put her hand on Maybelline's nose. She looked Maybelline in the eye and said, "You are a very nice-looking horse. You are the nicest-looking horse I have ever seen. Of course, I have never seen a horse before. But I have seen a pig. There is a pig who lives on this street. I know that pigs and horses are not the same at all. Other than that they both have hooves. Even though they are different kinds of hooves. You have very nice hooves, by the way."

Maybelline twitched her ears this way and that. She let out a pleased-sounding chuff of air.

"Stella!" shouted a boy. "Stella, watch out. Horses can be very dangerous. They can kick out suddenly with their hind legs and harm the unsuspecting."

"That's my brother, Frank," said Stella to Leroy. "He worries a lot."

Maybelline put her nose up in the air. She sniffed. She whinnied and put a question mark at the end of the whinny.

"What you are smelling is toast," said Stella to Maybelline. "Every morning, Mrs. Watson makes toast for her pig. Mercy is the name of the pig, and she is a pig who likes toast with a great deal of butter on it. Have you ever had toast with a great deal of butter on it? It's very good."

"Wait a minute," said Leroy Ninker. "Is this Deckawoo Drive?"

"This is Deckawoo Drive," said Stella.

"I have been here before," said Leroy.

And just as Leroy Ninker finished saying these words, a woman stepped out on the front porch of the house next door.

She was holding a butter knife in her hand, and a pig was standing beside her.

"Good morning, Stella," called the woman. "And Mr. Ninker! It is lovely to see you again."

"Hello, Mrs. Watson," said Leroy Ninker. "I would like for you to meet my horse, Maybelline."

"Well," said Mrs. Watson, "what a wonderful horse. She looks like a true equine wonder. You must both come inside and have some toast."

"But I don't know if Maybelline will fit through the door," said Leroy.

"Oh, heavens," said Mrs. Watson. "There is always a way to make things fit. Come inside, come inside."

"Come on," said Stella. She took hold of Leroy's hand.

Leroy turned to his horse. He said, "Come with me, horse of my heart. We are going to eat some toast."

The cowboy started to walk.

The horse followed along behind him.

The cowboy and the horse went inside.

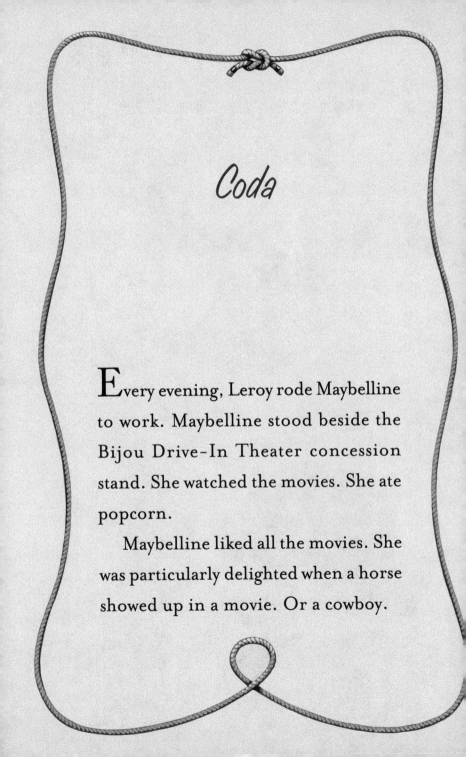

Coda

Every evening, Leroy rode Maybelline to work. Maybelline stood beside the Bijou Drive-In Theater concession stand. She watched the movies. She ate popcorn.

Maybelline liked all the movies. She was particularly delighted when a horse showed up in a movie. Or a cowboy.

But Maybelline's favorite movies were
the love stories. She put her ears up in
the air and listened very closely to the
beautiful words that people said to each
other. As they spoke, she nodded and
nickered quietly.

The horse was happy.

She knew that late at night, on the way home from the Bijou, Leroy would speak to her. Word after beautiful word would come from the cowboy's mouth, from his heart.

And in the darkness, underneath the bright stars, Maybelline would listen to them all.

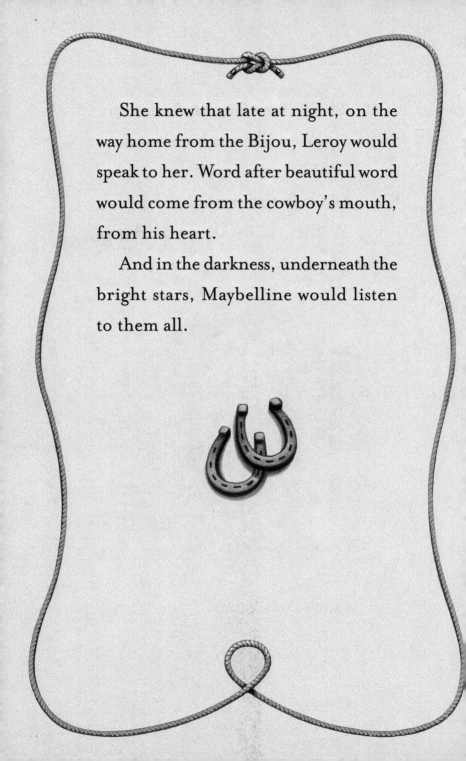